AF347663

INSIGHT PUBLICA
®

Nadakkavu, Kozhikode, Kerala, 673011
www.insightpublica.com
e-mail: insightpublica@gmail.com
SHINE IN LOWLAND
Nabilah Haniph
(English)
First Edition: November 2021
Copyright © Reserved
All rights reserved.

ISBN 978-93-5517-103-0

SHINE IN LOWLAND

Nabilah Haniph

Shine in Lowland is my first anthology of poems. This collection consists of my pickled thoughts arranged in strands and most of it was written during my early years of puberty. The verses are diverse in its content and topics range from contemplation and sorrow to love for nature, nation and infatuation. The damsel in me had a confused upbringing which reflects in my versification too, most of it looms around sorrow, solitude and confusion. The second part of this anthology will definitely consist of more love poems which will have shades of longing and desertion. Shine in Lowland is a tomb dedicated to my lost love that had to die young due to unwanted space given to undeserving persons and opinions. The world has always been unjust to lovers and poets, me being both, had to suffer the brunt twice.

Having been a vagabond gypsy all throughout and leading an unsettled life, it took more than a decade for me to publish my first anthology. Yet, the poet in me is unrest and I wield my pen whenever I am in despair. The love for words is platonic and the spatial years have been witnessing my verses root, enroute and uproot the various incarnations of me and finally making me believe in myself and let the world see my creations.

My poems are the result of the books I was
encouraged to read in my childhood and early
adulthood by my late grandfather, Vaidyanveetil
Noordinkunju Rawther. On this day, when my
words get printed in black and white, I fondly
remember him and feel blessed to have borne
his genes for literature. I had lots of inhibitions in
showing daylight to the diary which contained
my poems. And today, thanks to a handful of
good friends, I got it done. Thank you, Lal Deni
for encouraging me to get this in book form. My
love and gratitude to my family, especially my
husband, Jaison Augustine, who believes in me
more than I do and my greatest fan, my daughter,
Iffah Maryam.

Nabilah Haniph

email: nabilah.haniph@gmail.com
website: shineinlowland.com
facebook & instagram: Nabilah Haniph

FOREWORD
BY PRABHA VARMA

Nabilah's 'SHINE IN LOWLAND' is a brilliantly crafted collection of poems that transcends the barriers of nation states and appeals to the poetry loving people around the world. The beautifully conceived collection directly converses with the changing sensibility of the readers of different generations.

Her poems stand apart with their nobility of thoughts, originality of images, beauty of stylistic narration, depth of insights and the vastness of farsightedness.

The collection makes a good read and takes the readers to a higher realm of sensibility, and unscaled heights of experiences.

The poet has her own unique ways of expressing what she sees behind common sights and what she conceives beyond the ordinary level of conception. She dwells on a wide range of topics and comes out in flying colours, churning the complexities of human predicament.

She makes use of a poetical language which filters and heightens the current language and beautifies it with the sporadic sprinkling of the subtle nuances of verses and striking images. It seems she is convinced about the therapeutic value of poesy and she successfully employs a plethora of innovative images that pacify the bruised souls to a great extent. The serene mind of the poet gets truly reflected in what she scribbles down! Her concern about humaneness, which is being done away with at a faster pace deserves special mention. She seeks to measure the distance between a homosapien and a human being and the distance gets marked in her poems in its totality.

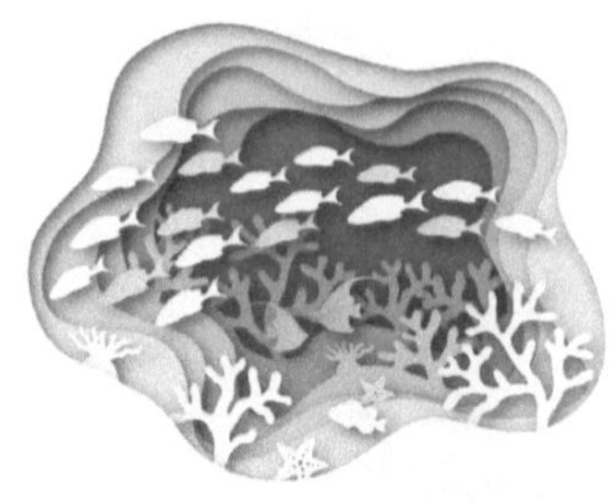

CONTENT

THE LEASE OF LIFE

Glory is for Him.
Who wins a battle by Himself
And here I stand
Aimless in the battle field
Death creeps and crawls
Ready to pounce anytime
But fate protects me and
Asks my fortunes in return.
Fortune and pain are destined
In life of every man.
Warriors overcome hurdles

I remain at the starting point
thinking the path is too risky.
This squabble life with no good
Is better to be surrendered to Him
than repenting of yesterday.
The life has set sail and
it will sail unto the shore
Even

If the wind loses his temper,
If the waves betray the boat
If the sail is seasick!
It keeps on sailing
To the horizon of life.
And may never rise again.

2003

THE SOUBRETTE

With long sighs I watched,
Great weary yesterdays.
Till yesterday I was
The idol of beauty,
The river of lust to
quench their thirst of eyes
They carved their lewd kisses
On the apples of mine

Their fetid breath
Mashed the rose on my face
and measured my breasts
At the brim of brandy
Nights devoid of sleep,
And my presence was their pleasure
'Somnolent eyes shone
Seeing me', quote they, lascivious
feeling feed the fire to flirt'
But today the autumn
Strained all my hues,
Base, brittle and brown
I stand so stupid to sex
Like the jasmine who
Smelled so sweet turned rotten,
Like the camphor burned to ashes.
Like a soubrette, I danced for them
And now like a sou, worthless to men.
Mirror, maid and money
Always minion to man!

2004

THE SORROW OF DEPARTURE

I know there's a life for all
Even for the rich and the ruined
For young and old, men and all
To dine with the Goddess of death.
She comes to all whenever
None know (some know) to them
To invite to her kingdom of darkness
in a different form to all.
After the dinner all depart, some
Just stay wherever they are,
Some locate the road of darkness
With the light of goodness
Turning in their hearts!
Some stammer in the dark
And falls into pits for having no light
Oh Men!
Then why do you long
To live more when your end is near
Alas! None can ever miss Mother Death's kiss
One and only kiss on the breath
To put all the beings to sleep
A sleep where one never wakes!

●

2003

DAWN ON THE DALE

Leaving behind a night of taunting dream
That drains even the doze like a stream!
This house of mine was lone in the hill;
I left it asleep while I went for a walk
The laugh of the wind was worse than the chill;
Yet I waited in the wild waves of wind,
The lost beauty for the last two months was to find.

I could see in the blunt black sky a wriggling,
It was the bird in the cage that was struggling!
But lo! The sky now tore its night dress,
And above rises the rain of the repleted sun!
Long after the weary days of suppress;
O just behold the vale profound!
It shimmered like an antique chest of gold!

All the beauty buds bloomed to bow
The King the sands of bright blue above!
He rose up in the firmament sending his arrows,
Illuminating the sights hidden by the phantoms
For his grace, glare and glaze none could narrow!
He is the victorious warrior on the azimuth,
But at the horizon, dwindles like an infant to sleep!

2002

MOTHER AND CHILD

Child to a mother is
The purest form of happiness.
Her cradle of care
And the lullaby of love
Is all set apart for the
Lone heir of her milk.
Womanhood is woeful
Until her womb is filled
Her pains come to rest when
His smile sends the rays of
Hope and happiness to her heart.
Blessed are those who bear
These kings and queens of paradise.

Mother to a child
Is the idol of love.
She is the pujaari of
His temple of case and caress
His life is indebted to her
For each drop of milk his blood bear,
For she is the only court where
All his sins are forgiven.
Her lap is the softest pillow
And her feet are the heaven,
Where the angels shower their blessings
His life had the happiest moment when
He was gifted to her, her own.
Blessed are those, who are the
Sailors of the ocean of love.

2001

THE LONE WOODS

The lone woods of this forest,
Weeping silently, confessing
Its love to the whistling wind
Dancing and wriggling river
Strokes gently the wet lands
Of this reviving the soil beds
The sky and the green
Join hands with each other
and the horizon smiles at the mate,
the sun shines at their mate!

●

2004

JUST A MINUTE

Moments of joy
Limits the restriction
Yet the shadow of woe
Chase the hues of this love
How can time alter
And drive into both?

●

2001

STAR GAZER

The big ball of fire was
sinking in the sea of clouds
and light dispelled its
way for darkness.
All the visions
fluttered before my eyes.
The sluggish sky brought
the silvery moon beams
Around the ferny floor.
Silence was dispatched
All over the hedge; even
In my mind full of wandering thoughts!

For a minute, I held my
Hands onto the heart of nature.
A sudden ray of light made me
feel the Night's symphony.

I heard a gloomy song
Sung by an incongruous voice
Later found it as
The hoot of an owl.
But a truth lay in front of me

Very naked, the inconceivable fact,
An incoherent wailing
Of some incognito spirits,
Not visible in the moonlit sky.
The soothing songs of crickets buzzing,
and melodious music of night birds,
all made my heart fill with pleasure
except one, the one and only one:
The lonely star at the centre of
the blackish blue firmament
made me recollect all my memories.

The orphan asterisk
Whose face reveals all its woe
Apart from the tree, away from
The moon, far from all earthly joy,
stands afar this sole star.
Its sorrow and dismay
behind its radiant light.
So is the same, my story
Away from all earthly troubles
I seek protection at the foot
Of dark, night of nature.

●

2003

A SUPPORT

Once a magical music of a flute
Wafted through my ears
The music was thrilling .   it,
It was enchanting.
It evoked in me a divine spirit
And I set in search of the source.

The warble led me from my house
Through the green fields
Jeweled with ripened paddy
Across the wooden coconut bridge
To a dazing, dainty dale
And the cool air was embellished
By the enchanting music from the flute
The pleasant fragrance of the flowers

I followed my heart and it
still pursued the music.
For a moment, the movement
Of my heart stilled
And my eyes blinked.
I forgot the garden,
The world and myself
And immersed my mind
In the ocean of music and
The rising sun of beauty.
Yes. . . A youth
Whose eyes glittered
With the luminance of
A thousand rising suns
His chest revealed
All his machismo and valour

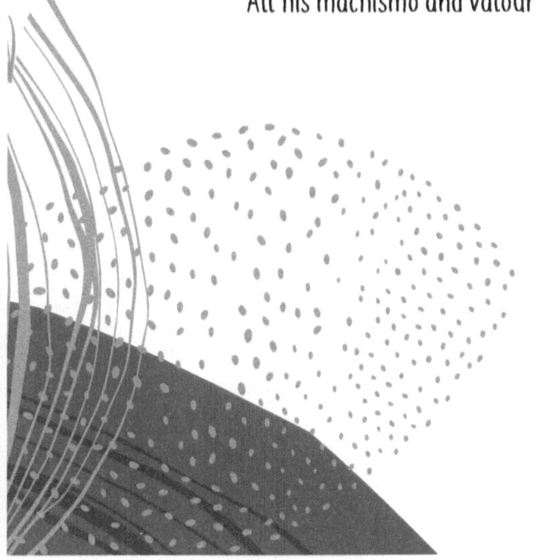

His dress was a
Elegant as his flute
And his hair shined
Brightly even in mute

At the first sight, my heart
Got stuck to his like a magnet.
Surely was he
A source of attraction
And a stripling of beauty.
Mine and my own
Dwell guy of dreams
His looks were charming
His heart was dancing
Like a peacock before his mate,
It all impressed mine.
He was a man of charisma
But missing was something
On his face that left me
wholly in chaos.
What??
Something drew closer to him
Me, my heart and my love

Seeing me, he for something
Searched; his support, his stick
He took it and tried to
Stand by himself, but
Oh his hands weren't firm
But my hands were
Too was my mind and decision
To give him support-
Physically, mentally and morally
Became my vow
Later, came to my mind
The whole woeful tale
That his heart shared with mine
His stay was of solitude
Same as me—an orphan
The charm and grace was not needed
But healthy limbs to support!
His parents regarded him useless,
And his siblings went to play
Leaving all hint alone.
From his childhood all
That he possessed and
His support were just turn—

The flute to suppress his woe
And the stick to suppress his misfortune
But now I made a promise
Not to leave him anywhere,
And to make him a part of mine.
Now I found the missing piece
On his face - a smile.
It broke out with the scintillation
Of a hundred fireworks in the sky
We both were happy
And led towards life, him
With my mind and person, in hand.
Now the end of came out
Of this millennium love story
That we lived happily thereafter.

●

2002

LOVE MESH

The fire lit in a loving heart
Is fiercer than that in a haystack!
The tempest of a longing soul
Is more waffling than that of a rose!
The joy of the merging mates
Is more soothing than that of the
music born on the flute's mouth!

●

2003

TWILIT GLOOM

The light residing in me is dwindling
as the spring departs from nature.
The springtide blooms
Are losing its fragrance and all.
Words fear to come out, and
Ink refuses to pour the feelings.
Extravagances blinding lyrics
Causing convulsion to my dreams
My mind is wandering like a squabble
In a universe of intense romance,
But finds void in paper.
I'm in a mad storm of dilemma
Lucidity in poem is hazy
The light over the moor,
Is glimmering and glazing
Still is waiting for mating of
Words and emotions and
seeping of spring from twilit gloom.

2003

VISION TODAY: 3000 AD

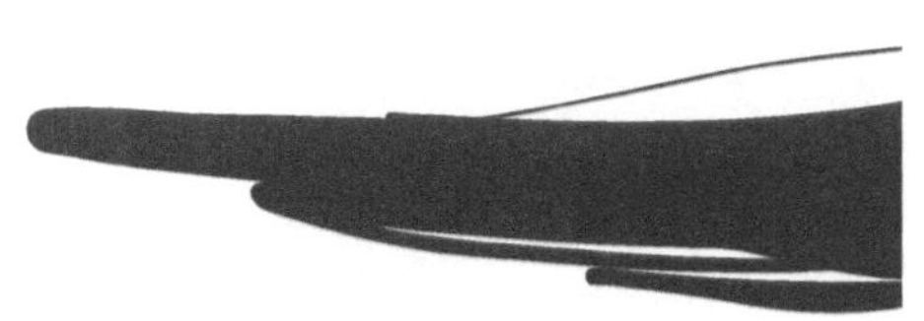

Yesterday I laughed at time,
Creeping slowly behind me.
Yes, I derived my heart's desire,
I defeated time, ahoy
In the race of yesterday
I travelled faster than time,
Then making jests, well, at time.
Yet only today I realized
Time defeated me,
I returned to my past
Stones and stills came to my side
But where am I?
An infant to the newly wedded
Earth and time,
Oh mother, forgive me
I killed you!
Oh father forgive me
I defeated you
No my destiny
Yesterday I laughed at
The ramps and ruins of my genes
I'm reborn to repent
The sins and sorrows of survival.
Oh parents please forgive
This pathetic parasite!

2001

WAIL OF A WAIF

I see myself among
The endless series of
Stars as a pale dark
Moonlight by else standing
Different and odd

Right from infancy
Sorrow was my shadow
Nights were less where
I have wept little
The war took away
My father and the society
Destroyed my mother
All my siblings were
Vanquished by epidemic.

Yet fate left me
All alone among aliens
And God punished severely
By fuelling the fire

I wandered everywhere
As a stray not a place to rest

Found joy everywhere but
Me not suitable there
I feel everywhere a void!
The storm of sorrow
And the tempest of troubles
Blew off all the light of hope
Shut all the open windows
And shattered all my dreams

Everywhere I found taunting
Laughs and some sympathetic faces
But no helping hands
As a child found
Every way possible difficult
For the daily bread

The people who care for us are none
Those who help us are few
But the whole society regard
Us united — "ORPHANS"
But why are we orphans?
The society seized our rights
And left us sole uncaring
And helpless — we ORPHANS!

2004

INDIA

From the abode of snow
Till the huge water body
Lies a heavenly garden.
A land of amazing extremes!

Up stands the Himalayas,
The crown that embellish her head
Down flows the Indian Ocean
Cleans her Virgin foot

Enchantment is everywhere:
In the rushing Ganges,
In the tree muffled woods,
In the ripen golden paddy fields!

The land at whose lap
The history sleeps
The land whose liberty
The foreign perils muffed

The reverent vigorous rivers
Flow as her untainted blood
And that virgin blood of valor, struggle
And patience flow through the body of her children.

The chanting of mountain fills
Its atmosphere with glory and reverence
The fraternity among the countrymen
Even ashamed the angels in the heaven

The jewels of peace, freedom,
Equality, brotherhood and spirituality
And held high in minds
And views of every patriot, every Indian.

Our past was struggle filled
Our present is laborious
Yet the future to come
Surely be extorted and glorious.

2001

FOR YOU, FRIEND

Like the autumn leaves, years teemed down
Yet the reminiscence remains.
A token of love for my dear friends who all leaving
the school this year

Once in my life I was alone
then you came smiling to me
your blushing face filled my solitude
with our houses so near,
from the second year of schooling,
the winding path back home
from school was bright and cheery
from fun to fights.
From chocolates to dreams,
We grew into the priming teens.

A friendship unsoiled
so deep in the hearts,
often unsaid in present,
I could read your eyes
and you hear my heart.
Never have you said
a word to pinch me
and your worries and loves
came into my silence.

I see the path back home,
from school so dry and windless:
how much had we laughed-
the jests in tuition classes
the jibes on juniors
the fine mimics in physics lab.
the day when we perched

under one umbrella,
those rainy days will be never more.
eight years of togetherness-
a friendship notable.

Today destiny stands there,
and the day to part is so near
calling you to a world so new
And amidst strange faces,
promise me you shall never sob
and struggle to succeed,
days of golden memories
can be treasured
A dream of teeming arts
is to be treasured.
Good bye friend!
Good luck!

●

2003

Treasuring the love you gave me,
your friend.

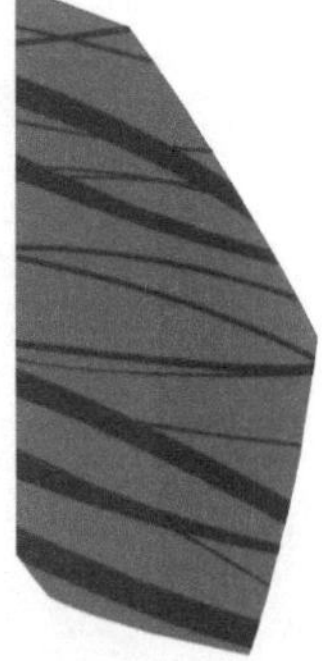

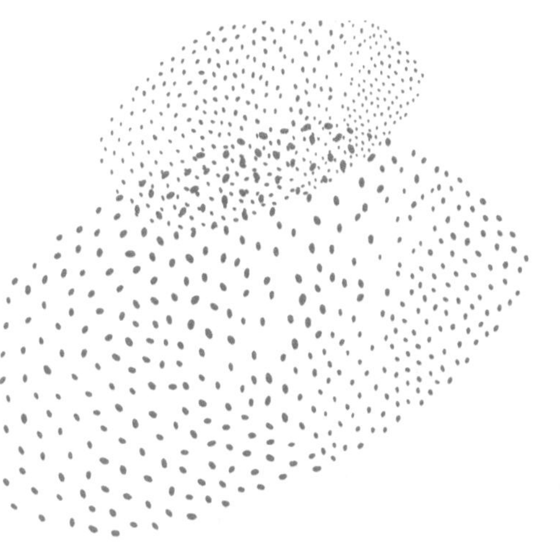

THE EMPERORS OF THE SKY

The sun sank into
the sea hiding its light from dark
And the reddish firmament was
at last conquered by the night
The sun was vanquished from the field
and the moon came riding in his chariot
with his uncountable warriors.

All the beings of earth were in gay
and welcomed the new ruler of sky.
The trees swayed and danced
with the music of the whistling wind
The crickets painted the mute
With its buzzing sounds.
The night birds' hoots were in pace

with the incongruous whispers
of the phantom spirits that wander
with the night kind and his kinsmen.
The earth presents the vintage to the
conquerors of the endless kingdom of clouds,
from the fresh blooms of spring dale
the moon and the stars were overwhelmed
by the razzmatazz of the earth beings.

All the stars drank the drink
and went to sleep, unaware
of the sedative trap concocted
by the day God and earth beings
Now the moon was all alone in the sky
and the sun rose from his hideout
sending the thousand arrows of light
at the lone ruler and warrior in the sky.
The rays of light pushed the drunken
king and courtiers out of the kingdom,
and embellished the sun as the emperor.
The whole sky was scintillated by the light
rays and the blooms blossomed in gay
revealing hues of joy, love and refreshment

men bowed with respect and set to work
and beasts engaged their time in business
Yet again in the evening
the moon attacks and vanquishes
them and in morning the sun rays clear them.

Nature never worries on it.
She knows that both are her dear ones
her love for both is equal, then
why should they fight for the firmament?
So she gave the day sky to sun and
at night the moon became the king.
This keeps them unharmed while
they attack each other.

2003

MY LADY LOVE

Oh how I envy you,
damsel of yawning day,
deity of drowning dusk!
for the past springs
we were together,
Total strangers.
And today before me,
my lady love,
in priming youth stand.
What shall I give you? –
to please your lips
to entertain your eyes
to seek that smile.
Shall I grab the shine of stars,
the lust of trees,
the glade of brooks
or the ruby of my heart?

Tell me dear,
or whisper to the wind.

For every bell
We were together
yet your beauty
never struck before me.
What shall I sing to you
My ladylove? -
To soothe your ears
To summon my love
To living your heart?
Shall I bring you
the rock of rocking seas
the cries of craving caves
the jingles of joking jungles
or the melancholy strain
of this grieving poet?

Tell me, sweetheart
Or confess to the moon over the moor.

My every dream is yours-
Mistress of mute and my mind
On every thought of you,
I spur like a madman,
How shall I show you, beauty?
the wild waves of my woe,
my vast ocean of love,
my beseech for you?
Shall I throb my heart with a dagger
cut down the doze, dear for you
or tear apart my chest before you?

Please fill my void with you,
Kill my dreams without you.

●

2003

FOR THE SONS OF EARTH

I see those free birds
stooping to conquer
the horizon of sky,
I remember those men
barred behind the bars
of limitations, they chained to the sins of
traditions that pull back
the unveiled evils.
Men, I see those woods
through the window
lashing and hashing in the wind;
The silence of eeriness,
The warble of the wild

and the gladly gushing brooks,
I remember the clotted
ideas of men, why do
they sell their brains-
to taste their lavish life?
Why do they hand their heart-
to stay their brother's desire?

Let me sing
a solo so somber
for the sons of earth
the lovers of life
its little of jest
for before the light dwindles,
let you not lament on your lies
for the last catch
and the lost chance
spares only losses!

●

2001

A MESSAGE FOR MAN

Alone I sat
measuring the horizon.
The world of waves rippled
at my foot, the browning breeze
kissed gently at my cheeks

for a moment, the azimuth
became a window,
every element evolved at élan
but my mind swam deeper.
The foams of sea,
The clouds of sky,
The blooms of beauty,

The sigh of breeze,
all for once
smiled at me.

I applauded and
praised their prospects
but what they said
were more than dreams,
Sweet springs and
bitter autumns,
morning monsoons and
biting winters
all aren't new to them.
But their friends are
slayed by man.

Hardships can have an end
but pride ends only in ruins.
Here the race is from man to man
where he goes—who can guess?

My heart sank with sun
in the sea of dismay,
Shame, madness and woeful worries.
Oh where did our fraternity hide,
there dies all in the battle in blood
none gain nor none gays
only that gusty gale prevails.

Stop it, at least for time's sake,
where we go, all we know, but
grace, gold and glory, where do you take?
Where your corpse lie decayed
or to hell, where your souls decay?

●

2004

WHAT MAMMA SAID

The child with his mother
sat under the tree in the garden.
A cute but perplexed child
looked above his mother's
gentle and affectionate face.
The boy said: "Oh: what a pretty
little garden full of flowers fresh"
"Yes so is also our life a bed
of roses with thorns hidden beneath.
So in life understand my dear,
make it as fanciful as these roses
Yet take care for the troubles hidden,"
came the mother's reply to the question.
"Oh mum look how quietly do
the lizards tries to catch his prey,
over there?" asked the child curiously.
"Yes, it's the behavior of all men

creeps and crawls to his enemy
and give off an attack suddenly
for the world likes success but not
successful people so the wise does
the same as the fly did,
fly off for the lizard cannot!"
was the mother's remark to her lad.
"Mum, spring is very nice indeed
after all the chilling? Cold winter.
It has made my mind fresh for
it is the season I love the most!"
chuckled the child at the chirruping
birds. "Very good my dear," stated mum
"Be optimistic always, think
That for every bad there's a good,
Like the sun dispels darkness away!"
Taking no notice the boy cried,
"Look mum, a gleaming cobweb,
and look at the spider, he's a good hunter!"
"Yes and look how he struggles
to finish the frame of his web."
Paused the mum and gently stroked his hair,
"The spider shows us the way

to the kingdom of success where
few people only reached and to
find the road is not impossible.
Mission may mock at you but
don't give up saying impossible,
for hardwork is the torch that
lightens our way to success.
so my dear, success is the only
one of the diamond in knowledge."
said the woman to her child on her
lap who had already fallen into sleep
she gently kissed his forehead
and smiled and winked at the wind.

2001

THE TWILIT HOURS

When at evening
the sun receives its
farewell party,
there ends up
an episode of hurry.

The twilit dim climbs down
and the night shadow
grows larger and stronger.
The trees down the valley
lined as in march parade, purple.
The livid hues of day
all dry and dirt filled
hazy in the dusty atmosphere.

The thirsty earth craving
for water all day
and we fight the heat
so high and red
in ACs and coolers
the fan for me and you
and a hand fan or
a dhoti for poor man's sake
but the much better
for the droopy birds
over the brooding tree
as if about to fall
like its dry paper leaves.
Muscles ache right
at the middle of day
and an afternoon nap
isn't a bad idea.
Gharwali ladies
after their noon shower.
So a fresh start their
talk on things
those less matter less to all
but great to them.
The non-stop debate
with one hand on hair

busily combing their
long tresses and scent
of prickly heat talc
reverberate in the rough air.
Except for beads of sweat
or the ever leaking
corporation pipeline
there is no scope of water
even for the craving earth.

Yet evenings bring
a new story to us.
The scent of wet earth
and the first rain
are so both rare and fine.
The long day scorching
 oohs and aahs turn
into whistles of children
playing a hundred games
without a break.
It's happy having evening tea
with Papa after
coming from his office.
There is a hurry
even for the gloomy birds

to reach their homes,
to meet their dear ones.

The twilit hours
In blues and purples
And the silhouette of
The bidding day and
The budding night
is a sight so unforgettable
like the whisper of
newlywed couples
giggling, seen clearly
among the wriggling of
the wine red clouds.
The first hours of night
is the spirit that flushes
in the nerves giving
stamina for nothing
but rest yet
a placid walk of sky
is what we see everyday
and when she takes rest
its twilit hours.

●

2002

MEMORIES

They are those living feelings
that breathe even when buried
that glow even when burned.

Its like the blood that flows
out through my eyes.
I hardly collect them
So they fall on bare earth
And I can see her heart hurting.
Sorry, I never wished so
but your children weep
and tears their yesterday
like tears on to you.

But you- feel it
fuel it and flourish in it.
Oh my, green memories,
I wish I could tell you.

Everyone has a story to tell,
a life to weave
a saga to sing
-each so different in size and style
I hear them-
or seem to hear them
for like to hear them,
I like to lend them my ear.
So that I may hear them,
my heart may know them.

Just because we're born to two
and have to live as two
we can't see others two,
for the eyes we have are two
but what we see are not two

my ink may fill the space
and the words fill the lines
but my mind is void
and what shall I fill it with?

the songs I sang were so somber
the tunes I turned were too tattered
the verses woven were worn out
my heart longs for change
my words long for change
I could find for a change
if and only if my mind
dotted with idealistic ideas,
could come out of the contemporary.

●

2004

REMINISCENCES

The hands of time
take me to the past.
Back to my school days
- that'll never return.

After the month of May
shall start the hectic year
Exams, homework and projects
adds weight to studies
and the 1.5 kg small fluty organ!
But there come friends,
P.T. and holidays to
camouflage my worries and grief.

The school taught me that
Yesterday was but a dream
Tomorrow is only a vision.
But a well-lived today
Makes
Every yesterday a dream of happiness

and every tomorrow a vision of hope.

The school made me walk
through the roads of success
and made my mind and foot
firm in views and ways

Today my life is void without them
but every moment I feel my
heart playing and rejoicing
on the shores of childhood.
Its long since those moments
have left me alone.
Memories are like dreams
but which are sweet, last longer
an impression engraved
in fathoms of my heart
—the Reminiscences.

●
2005

FLOWERS

The symbol of beauty
the expression of love
are what we call
nothing else but flowers.

They adorn the ferny floor
make happy a wanting heart
feel contended a glittering eye,
it's the jewel of the Nature.

They are the smile seen
on the face of a five year old.
They are the ornaments that
embellish the bride Nature.

The thorn that attracts
the bees to embrace them
are what we call
nothing else but flowers.

2001

THE SPRING'S CALL

The golden rays of the daystar
came streaming on to her,
unfolding her wintery raiment
and adorn her in haughty hues.

The trees stand in their spring livery
bidding bye to the biting winter
and the hedge coloured in dappled green.
The winds took away all the fallen leaves
and the trees refreshed themselves
with a bath of brisk morning rays.

The rivers are overwhelmed
with both water and wayward.
The water waves wave and
wriggle with the warning wind.
They feel happy and relieved after
grappling with long frozen slavery.

The Spring is never complete
without the spring blooms.

The wafting fragrance evokes
bliss and blithe in all.
The lavenders blossom to lavish air
and the roses and tulips garnish the garden.

The spring is the harmony of flowers
chrysanthemums, crocuses and carnations
dainty daffodils embellish the morning hours.
The spring never ends in these.
It's the victory over harsh and
ungracious circumstances in nature!

2002

THOSE ROSY FANCIES

There was a time,
when roses were dearest
To me . . .
and you were dearest
to me . . .
The roses you gave me
I treasured in my heart
the kisses you gave me
I treasured in my eyes.
The days we spent in
the shadow of the twilight
and the dreams we wove
together at the foot of the beach.

There was a time,
when roses were dearest
to me . . .
and you were dearest

to me ...
Then came the autumn so fast,
and roses became pale
and you drew from me ...
for
like leaves fall, years died
and you, like the withered roses
decayed and died in my heart.

There was a time
when roses were dearest
to me ...
and you were dearest
to me ...
today, you are so close
but intimacy is lacking
life had taught me so much
that love was only to
be forgotten like sweet dreams
we depart, like never met
strangers ...
without a smile ...

●
2004

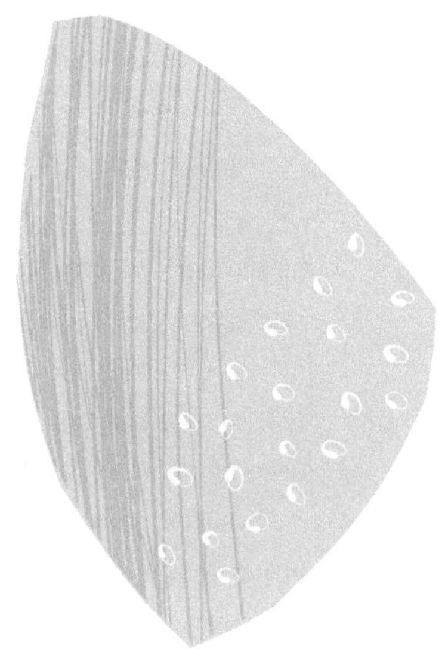

THE HEAVE OF
THE HAPLESS

Every evening
when the sun retires
after his job of distributing
rays of light to men,
there sets inside my mind,
the tires of a persnickety day
and in rises along with
the night queen,

my peripatetic companions
invading my minds and plundering
my tedious thoughts,
it, like a seductive drug crops
a new voluptuous spirit in me.
The twinkling sparks of the night sheet-
among which resides the votive lives
of my life donors,
reveals their life over there.
They show me their blinking eyes
and hands calling me for a visit
and as a permanent guest to
the guild of wandering phantoms.

I've wished a thousand times
to leave my name and person here
and mix among the infinite unnamed
untamed lovers of eternity and peripheral.

2005

A WORD
ON A WORLD

This world is so strange
everything seems to be sanctimonious-
Mystery unfold deep beneath everything.
The term in earth is so short
yet every being loves to live long.

Look for the blossoms
that bloom with the sun rays of spring
and leave all its lovely leaves on earth
when departs its soul at spring's death.
It does know that it has
to but leave its beloved body
but never forgets to flower
and spread its fragrance all over.

Take a glimpse on that candle flame
that burns with a bright light
and sacrifice every cell of its body
to envelope the draining darkness
and lead the right way,
it does know that its life
dwindles as it share its light
but never hesitates to be lighted
and spread its light all over.

Look at those dappled green trees
that smile and sway in the gentle breeze
of the spry spring yet he know
autumn will make him nude.
He does know that the winter would
seize away his hair and hide his charm
but he never worries on it on spring
and never waives to give shade to one
but spreads his hands all over.

Take a glance of the gushing river
that dances down the meadow 'n moors.
She never craves to desert the land

but never cries to depart the land
when she reaches the mouth of sea.
She does know that she has
to but leave her lover land
and join her siblings in the sea.
She drains and drenches the ground
and spread her spirit all over.

These all live for the moment
but manage to make the minion tenure
on this mysterious world but to
be productive and prolific to people.
They don't die off among dangers
but hopefully unite for time to heal
we man are a very young student
who should learn from these,
and spread our wisdom all over!

●

2004

THE MIRAGE OF MIND

A lover has reborn in myself
yet it's still not clear whether
the love of mine beseeches for a mate
or thirsts to give birth to a new romance.
Mute carries his song of love
Blank sheet paints his face.
Though not the idol of beauty
his eyes shimmer in my heart.
A panting thought delivers his smile
where my eyes blind his vision,
and sometimes his blind my thoughts.
This silly infatuation
may end any moment; when
another sculpture of elegance

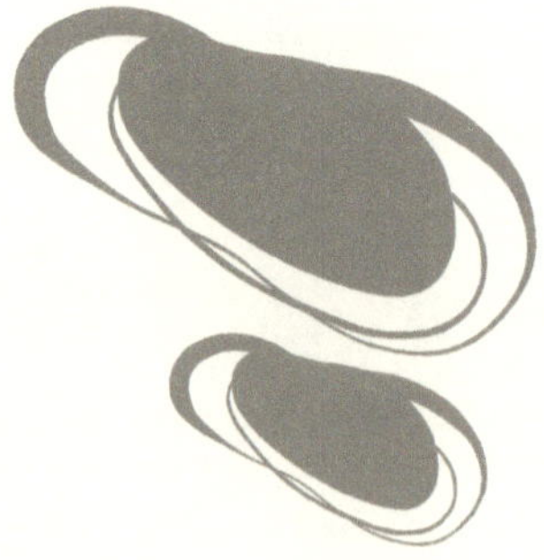

rises in mind of mine or his
'cause this immature affinity
pierces into our todays
—that goes in two different paths
forcing to magnetize each other
while we, trying hard to repel.

Love tries to dissuade one from his path
and persuade to mould into trouble
It shares pains and panics and pays back
the thirst for sullen 'mischiefs'.
Love induces a suggestive thought into one
and suffers over the whole of nerves.

How is love so great when
it delivers an agitation in thoughts
and simply make a menace in dreams?

2004

WHAT IS THIS HAPPENING?

Earthed dreams are budding again.
broken wings are spreading again.
The waves slept in my heart
why is it storming in my eyes?
Why is his face glistening
 in my love?

The torn papers are uniting . .
The shattered glasses are uniting . .
The broken love is uniting . .
Bind it, Blind it
don't forgive it, forget it.
Don't dance to it,
pause the verse.
Control it, suppress it! Damn it!!

●

2003

THE SOUL'S REPLY

No, no my damsel,
you never knew anything
I am a wanderer of ages —
since life had evolved
the creator created mates,
since birth and death became friends.

You are an infant before love
and everyone in the world is
the same as you.
You've never tasted this elixir of love,
'Very deceitful and rancorous' says
that wise and experienced lot.
Like a spider-woven web it lures
poor beings into his web and
later leaves them desperate amidst
the ocean of traumas where only a few escape.
It's a tactful glimmer of pain
never it joins a bond or
gives peace and joy to the two.
With the tempest of sorrow it
would wash off the mud castle made
of high hopes and tastes
and tatter and shatter all sweet dreams.

Then why the youth run behind
this indelible stain, blind?
Which do not give any indemnity
to the broken hearts,
tattered dreams
and shattered future?

Adam and Eve were the first to be loved
and as ages changed, love created
new relations among few.
Majnu faced it-who beseeched for Laila
Ranjha for his beloved Heer,
the same was for Romeo whom Juliet longed-
And it evolved Today to a new era
of swiftness and glints of modernism.

Dazzling smiles and conjuring eyes
all hoax gullible guys and gals
and useless mock after sometime.
It's just like the blazing rainbow
which after the rain vanishes among
the clouds of neverness.

It has benefitted none and none gained
except the broken L-O-V-E.

The anti-thesis of mankind has
given birth to hatred, lust and enmity
and will once provoke the main
reason for withering mankind.

But love is not mere blandishments
nor expressed in a blaze of colours
Love is not contented in gifts
nor dims after an age.
It's the constituent of men's blood
and the heart whispers every time it beats
Love is deep below one's mind and
none is able to hap the depth.
It's a bond of emotions plus reality
yet most forged to the latter
and the hurdles head here.
They universe themselves in dreams
and leaves reality- the vital vitamin
needed for life, love and life (progress)
Emotions constitute less love alone
but with reality blended together.
To reality, love is an adhesive link,
the cup of sweetness of life!

●

2003

THE FIRST LOVE

(Dedicated to my dearest friend on her first love)

My mind loves to wander
wide in the wayward world.
It's my dreams that give
wings to my words.
While sinking in sweet slumber
or resting with rest of the world
I don't float through those pages;
but sometime at his sight
I lose quite some of my chords
of contacts with this conceiving world.
Though those times were forgotten,
forced to forget with pain hidden
by none but me, my conscious.

Now whenever I see him
with my heart not running to his,
there's something that hurt me,
hinders me because:
It was a love of not two symbolic beings
but a bond of two unbound souls,
stray souls — in a sense
we were not persons to be met
yet we met
we were not persons to be loved
yet we loved.
Silent and sincere love
that runs not in eyes
but in nerves

which still heart burns
and the ember glows in pain
for even when the chapter is closed
my heart still bears his picture.

I do not seek for suggestions
but only support
I do not seek anymore his love
but only his presence
because it gives me pleasure
hard to say-
a parental protection.
Only thing I want from you
is nothing but your presence.
If you could sense it
please don't ignore me.
Because my love fonder
only when we are far
but turns friendship
when together.

2004

FRIENDSHIP

Friendship
It creates a deep
feeling in one's soul
It's something sacred and pure,
the simplest form of love
It's like a world full of joy
a bunch of roses
Which share its fragrance.
Friendship is sharing joy and sorrow
in a mixture of fun and fifths.
Friendship is nothing great
but grows on sharing.
Friends are made just
through a glittering smile from eyes
a word of encouragement in despair.

2001

A BIRTHDAY WISH

Like the lashing lovely lavenders let
this day define your delightful dreams
and awake, amalgamate and a mall all
your youthful yearn and yes to be yang.

Be the best blessings bestowed on you – I beseech
for one thing I wish you is :
The past portrays what you were
The present presents what you are
The future finds what you will be!
You are yourself
fight for the fiery fathoms
fly for the fleeing flocks of future
fund for the finest friendship to flourish.

●

2003

MUSIC OF THE SOUL

While gazing into pitch darkness
my heart was filled with sorrow.
I found my heart sinking down
in the mighty ocean of woe.
Tears rolled from my eyes
darkness enveloped my vision.
My life was meaningless
faults only I have made —
now the thoughts began to haunt
it pricked and pained my delicate heart.
No. This was unbearable.
I couldn't carry the burden of sorrow
it seemed to be impossible for
my heart to pound in second.

Suddenly an intense whisper was heard
my eyes stopped shedding tears,
my heart gave a long sigh.
It was a low incoherent sound
and the speaker was incognito.
I looked around the dappled green
and out the mystic blue firmament,
search above the sluggish lake
 and the towering brown mountains.
I stopped every deed and sharpened
my ears Trying to grasp the source.
I searched and listened
every mode and corner of the dale.
My eyes grew weary and
my heart began to set,
yet the source was not coming
onto my sense so
I closed page of my wild goose chase
and was about to return back.

Suddenly a moony beam took
myself somewhere,
I didn't knew where it was taking me

nor what its intention was.
I was dazed or rather bewildered
to be for a moment
in a dark, silent spooky nook
yet something was cutting the golden silence;
it found to be so familiar—
yes it was the very incoherent voice
of the incognito my heart rose
my eyes bloomed like a spring rose
and the euphony
turned out to a wondrous symphony.

The music seemed for me ethereal
it began to make all my feeling etiolate
and I was rafting in that marvelous melody.

The melody was more musical than
the mourn of a mountain mynah.
It enthralled all the cells
of my body like a lover-conjurer.

The music was more melodious than
the violent waves of the wavering waters

its tune had the acute conveyance
the departing leaves of lengthy winter
used to transmit.

The singer hid behind the veil of dark
but the voice bore the sweetness
 the early springtide rose's kiss-
the golden nectar bore.

The eyes swam in the oceanic music
and heart in that divine strain.
The music revealed before me
the great secret of life's sustainment,
the sustenance of truth
and the elixir of love.

The notes explained
'Love and Truth together
bound the eternity of life
Worldly delight and delusion with a body
never make man a complete
Life is a rainbow-vibrant in the sky
The seven hues of the Spectrum compress

Love — which embalm life
Truth — the true of Love and Time
Ethics — which embed reality in life
Beauty — that glows inside the heart
Realism — the chants that make life breathe
Sorrow — embedded as the shadow of life
Soul — the ember of life
That bolts life in security,
shadows wherever life goes.
Man is set free when life
is unlocked by the key of death.
Then the hues mix and wander
in the opacity of wild thoughts
through the vastness of universe.'

This song I repeat every time in dreams
yet not able to vocalize
when my mind is busy
and my brain on duty.
This music with nebulas meaning
holds his hand with Godliness.

●

2004

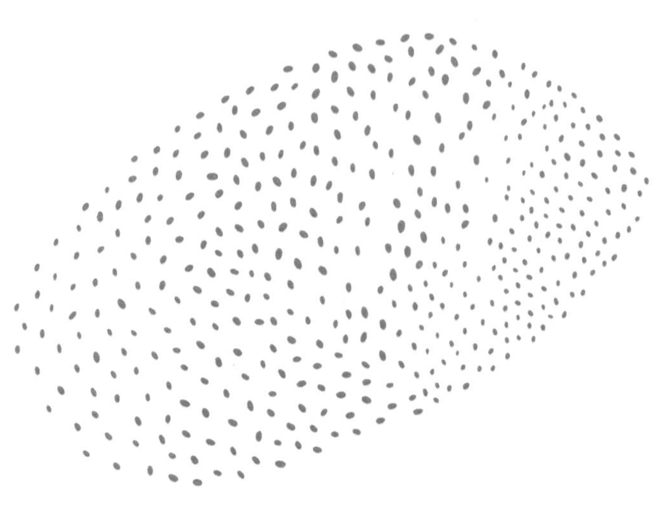

FOR DELIGHT

It was a moonless night,
I still remember, the day
we judged you were
born in me, Delight.

You came into our void life
like the first rays of dawn
you sponged the tears of our parents
like a rainbow in moody sky.
You were the answer — the find one
for the thousand prayers we made.

My spirits were delighted
when the reports sensed a girl

and it was we together
on that moonless night
named you, Delight.

You became the weight of all
like hornbill's prayer for vain
you became the eager of all
like the spring bells to bloom
you were for whom — the lucky one
 the whole house happily prayed for

My sadness was over
when my womb bore you
and it was we together
on that moonless night
made you the cradle, Delight

You became your mother's boon
like the light for leading path
you became your father's hope
like an angel hover everywhere
you where for whom/tuned-the last one
the wallaby of my love.

The scan report after 5 months
scared you had complications pre-birth
But it was my mind, all set
on that moonless night
to bear all pains for you, Delight.

You were told not to born on earth
as it was all the Hobson's choice
you were a firework unlit
as you had a place with the stars
you came to spread of glint of gay — the only one
and glided silently giving pain to all.

An unprecedented pain,
my abdomen pierced in vain
But the bleeding didn't stop my tears
on that moonless night
and you became a sweet dream, Delight.

You were an unborn boon to us
like the rainbow after the rain
you now were a dream in vicinity
like the mirage of Arabian Sands
you still adore not my womb — the unlucky one
but my whole now beseech for you

Though the nasty Today
shut the doors of Hope,
But the bosom of this hapless mother
on this moonless night
craves for you, Delight.

2003

DELUGE

Sitting on a poet's chair
with pens of different ink in hand
spontaneous emission of powerful thoughts
upon the paper, I could feel.
A world so new was open for me
where no chains nor pains could cut my sight
and I could sail to where my soul do dwell.

A poet sees not with eyes so fair
but his heart words the world in hand
Beauty, love and nature are just his thoughts
and with words all his pain he could heal
for the place he dwells for him is free
and never he blooms to see world's plight
where minds of men along with corpse swell.

Now it's my chance to find a pair
so that we could liftthe world with both our hands
and nurture values with words and thoughts
Let us nest an abode of peace with all our zeal
where the air to breath for man is free
of not smoke or smog but foes and fight
so that man could live a life of love and not in hell.

●

2004

THE POET OF TODAY

PART I
The doors of romance opened before me
and in glided the glade of a good morning

The flocks had flown early enough for the worm
and men started making hay when sun's warm

I could see foaming waves of the tempest ocean
gently kissing the sore or rocking the rocks

I measure the fathoms of the watery trenches
bring out sunshine the pearls of window

I silently walk with the silhouette of night
and kindle with the fireball of day

I run around splashing with moony rain drops
and behold the rainbow beyond the ferny floor drinking dew drops

I could see the horizon of the firmament
I could hearth jingle of the jungle brook

I could calm the storming sea into simple symphony
I could bloom the lamenting lilies to lovely lives.

I could pun the world of mine, paint the mute
I could away along with wind, water, waves and words

I am a poet of today I beseech a better tomorrow
for wish to grant our grandchildren a future without regrets.

Part II
I am a renegade of my age, I defy the idle idol
I am not servile to sermons, so they coined me atheist.

Yes, I am atheist, I shout to the sky shore and sea
I follow not what men say but mind say

I worship not the Lord in gold but the Lord in all

I read not the psalms in books but the psalms of love

I wield my pen for man to rise from ignorance
I yield my thoughts for relapse of renaissance

I stare at the universe not at void as they think
there I find everything and they find me insane.

I go against the tide, not the time
for those eyes behind me should see a world of man

I go stringing beads of mankind for our children
when they make chains around their necks and legs

I try to open those closed casements to the world in comb
and they sit inside the concrete rooms creating caskets.

I am a poet of today and I beseech a better tomorrow
for I wish to grant four grandchildren a future without regrets.

●
2005

A LAST WORD

I am ready to forget you,
If those fancy fairs fade their hue
for your heart I kept in mine
If you can take it back all's so fine!

As these waves roll on and on
so, my love flows on and on . . .

I am ready to forget you,
If not for my eyes you so sue
for your eyes did blaze in mine
If you can blow it out all's so fine!

As these gales blow on an on
so, my love flows on and on. . .

I am ready to forget you,
If that soul seeks something new
for your soul has not sunk in mine
If you can swim to shore all's fine!

As our life goes on and on
so, our love flows on and on . . .

2005

PAINS THAT PONDER

The drops fell all around
showing no mercy save me
for I was sparing myself
from those merciless pins of rain
under a silk umbrella.
That moment I mended the dogma
That rain's showers of blessing.

However hard I tried to hold
the umbrella above my head,
 the wind blew harder to divorce us.

And a mighty blow but to!
 Here I stand naked to the attack
my shield flew across the street
and I yelled at it in vain.

Trying to hide from those drenching pain
I moved a fast to a nearby shed,
lighted by a hole of dust.
Squeezing my all wet silk dupatta
I fathomed the dim lit shed,
half-eaten by rusty years,
smoked by bailing sun and blaze.

I could hear a faint mourn,
a feeble wail, first I thought
it some pariahs famished
but was misheard as it silenced
for I felt a consoling touch
that could but not stop the mourner
for the cry of hunger crakes
a kid astray
a man wild
a woman filth.

Yes as I moved closer to the voice
vicinity became lucid;
an abstract sensation flushed through me.

Behold the three,
left to be sons of street.
At the tender age when toys
should play in hands,
the tallest had rusty tongs.
When lollies adorn their
daydreams, they have
sorrow to fill void stomach
pain to heal hungry heart.

when there's the cold of rain
kids have blanketing parents
here these hapless ache
and tremble like the lone leaf
of the withered autumn tree.
As the three cradled to each other
like fallen drops on lotus lead
I moved towards them.

With raised hopes those
raised heads speared at me
and I smiled at them.
Those skinny souls had no
 smile to spare.
Dust and dirt covered
entire of their bodies even
in those watery eyeballs.

An innocence lingered
around the sooty bodies.
The filthy ground and
claustrophobic air, both
sensed the dwell of disease.

'God save these saplings
that the sowed in the street'.
And I extended a 10 rupees note.

For a moment,
darkness put off the light on face
as dismal sheen released from face
the sooty clouds departed

for the rays of redden shed sun
and I came out of the shed
I explored first the firmament
then the nearby bus stop
and slowly stepped onto
the dampened grass
that a tiny hand clasped
my silk dupatta from back
and I looked back,
and I was taken aback

The tallest of three, hardly ten
came up to me with the wet note.
He returned me the note of sympathy
asked demanded a job out of empathy.

From the stinking alley
his sound shook me.
For the first time in my life
I felt that pain can ponder,
filth can fancy
and sorrow and soul are same.

2005

CRYING FOR THE MOON

Silence slowly swept into my sleep,
 I became the witness to night's tantrums.
She shifted from side to side,
eyes on the mirror for the perfect look.
When I gazed at her black velvety locks
her eyes winked with a twinkle.
My dismal face was now lined
with a pearly luster of her love and light.
Her eyes met mine, I saw eternity.

A wave rippled at my foot
a storm roused in my heart.
Standing barely on the acme of
the monstrous rocks,
my heart cried for the moon . . .
when the raging waves mated
with the ravenous rocks beneath,
I held out my arms
and simply cried for the moon.

●
2005

SHINE IN LOWLAND

There is a place for all things to fall
in places it should be
after those fell apart.

The world dwindled in hours,
Cities a thousand miles apart
Were just a flight of few leaps
And I was in your arms.
The wait for more than a decade
Culminated in a smooch.

The runway lights of Mumbai glistened
In your eyes and together we saw
The iron birds take the flight
And land at intervals.
We sighed, smiled and soothed each other,
Time has gambled on our destiny,
And today, the forces that parted us,
Joined hands, spreadeagled its wings,
Brought us together,
as fast as wind could carry
up in this attic.

It was like yesterday, that I cried in your arms,
It was like yesterday, that I missed you a thousand times,
It was like yesterday, that I realised we belonged to each other.

My shine in lowland,
You will always remain
As the ember that still glows!
The spark, the smile, the silence and the sigh,
The sweat, the strokes, the solitude and the sorrow!

The world has a new meaning this morning,
Because destiny exists!
The days, the nights, the wind and the wine,
Nothing has ever been so alive,
Because love exists!
The fate bound us together
in the arms of this unpredictable world,
no matter what awaits us,
because miracles exist!
Finally, the bliss of seeing the pinnacle of pleasure,
In your eyes and falling like an autumn leaf
Into the folds of my fondle,
I realise, we exist!

●

2016